Ladybird  Readers

Puss in Boots

Picture words

boy

Puss in Boots

king

princess

mill

donkey

Ladybird Readers

Puss in Boots

Series Editor: Sorrel Pitts
Text adapted by Sorrel Pitts
Illustrated by Laura Barella

LADYBIRD BOOKS

UK | USA | Canada | Ireland | Australia
India | New Zealand | South Africa

Ladybird Books is part of the Penguin Random House group of companies
whose addresses can be found at global.penguinrandomhouse.com.
www.penguin.co.uk   www.puffin.co.uk   www.ladybird.co.uk

Penguin
Random House
UK

First published 2017
001

Copyright © Ladybird Books Ltd, 2017

The moral rights of the author and illustrator have been asserted.

Printed in China

A CIP catalogue record for this book is available from the British Library

ISBN: 978-0-241-28407-0

All correspondence to
Ladybird Books
Penguin Random House Children's
80 Strand, London WC2R 0RL

boots

partridge

ogre

carriage

married

castle

magic

Many years in the past, an old
man lived with his three sons.
When the father died, he left
his sons some presents.

He left his mill to the first son, and his donkey to the second son. He left his cat to the third son.

The cat's name was Puss,
and he could talk.

"Puss," the third son said,
"my brothers can make
money with their presents.
How can we make
some money?"

"Master, get me some boots and a bag," answered Puss.

The boy gave Puss some boots and a bag. Puss wore the boots, and he caught a rabbit in his bag.

Puss took the rabbit to the king.

"Here is a present from my master," said Puss.

"Thank you, Puss. But who is your master?" asked the king.

Puss had an idea. "He is the Lord of Carrabas," he said.

The next day, Puss went out with the bag, and he caught two partridges.

Puss took the partridges to the king.

"Here is a present. There
are two partridges from my
master, the Lord of Carrabas,"
said Puss.

"Thank you, Puss," said the
king. "I love eating partridges."

19

The next day, Puss and his master
were near a river. Puss saw the
king's carriage on the road.
The king and the princess were
in the carriage.

Puss had an idea. "Master," he said, "you must jump into the river."

Then, Puss ran to the carriage.

"Help me!" said Puss. "My master is in the river!"

23

"We must help the Lord of Carrabas," said the king. So, the king's men helped the boy out of the river.

"We must take you home," said the king. He put the boy into his carriage.

Puss ran in front of the carriage.
He saw some men working.

"The king is coming!" he said.
"Please say that the Lord
of Carrabas is your master."

"Who do you work for?" said
the king when he saw the men.

"We work for the Lord of
Carrabas," said the men.

The king's carriage left, and Puss spoke to the men.

"Who lives in that castle?" he asked.

"Our master lives there. He is an ogre," said the men.

Puss ran to the castle, and the ogre came to the door.

"Can I come in?" Puss asked.

33

"Come in," said the ogre, because he wanted to eat Puss.

"Can ogres do magic?" Puss asked.

"Of course! Look!" said the ogre. And he changed into a lion.

"Is that your best magic?"
said Puss. "Can you change
into a mouse?"

The ogre changed into a mouse.

37

Puss jumped on the mouse, and ate it!

A minute later, Puss heard people at the door.

When Puss opened the door,
he saw the king, the princess,
and his master.

"This is my master's castle,"
said Puss.

Soon, the princess and the boy
were married. They lived together
in the castle.

The boy, the princess, the king, and Puss in Boots lived happily for many years.

Activities

The key below describes the skills practiced in each activity.

Spelling and writing

Reading

Speaking

Critical thinking

Preparation for the Cambridge Young Learners Exams

1 **Look and read. Write the correct words on the lines.** 📖 ✏️

Puss   king   mill   donkey   boots

1 The first son's present
from his father.   mill

2 The second son's
present from his father.   _____

3 The third son's present
from his father.   _____

4 Puss wanted these
for his feet.   _____

5 A man who lives
in a castle.   _____

2 Look and read. Write *T* (true) or *F* (false). 📖

1 An old man lived with his
   three sons, but one day he died.   T

2 The old man left his sons
   some presents.

3 The old man left his mill
   to his first son, and his cat
   to his second son.

4 The old man left his donkey
   to Puss.

5 The old man's cat could talk.

3 Work with a friend. Talk about the two pictures. How are they different? Use the words in the box. 🗨

rabbit	castle	king	master
boots	bag	inside	grass

In picture a, Puss is with his master.

In picture b, Puss is with the king.

4 Find the words.

```
m  i  l  l  c  c  q  c  m
y  d  l  o  a  a  u  l  l
(b  o  o  t  s)  l  k  m  t
a  n  n  n  t  t  i  a  o
t  k  p  e  l  s  n  g  g
l  e  u  a  e  e  g  c  r
p  a  r  t  r  i  d  g  e
s  l  r  c  s  m  e  l  s
p  r  e  v  t  y  o  w  m
```

5 Look and read. Write *yes* or *no*.

1 Was the boy really the Lord of Carrabas?   no

2 Did Puss catch two partridges and take them to the king?

3 Did Puss and his master see the king in his carriage the next day?

4 Were Puss and his master near a castle?

5 Was the princess with the king in the carriage?

6 **Look at the picture and read the questions. Write the answers.**

1 Where were Puss and his master?

They were near a river.

2 What did Puss see?

3 How many people were inside the carriage?

4 Who helped Puss's master?

7 Read the text. Choose the correct words and write them on the lines.

1 can		must to	must
2 jumped		walked	swam
3 Excuse you!		Help me!	Thank you!

Puss had an idea. "Master," he said,

"you ^{1} _____must_____ jump into

the river."

The boy ^{2} _____ into the

river, and Puss ran to the carriage.

"^{3} _____" said Puss.

"My master is in the river!"

8 Ask and answer questions about Puss with a friend. 💬 ❓

1 *Why did Puss take a rabbit and two partridges to the king?*

Because he wanted the king to like his master.

2 Why did Puss tell his master to jump into the river?

3 Did Puss want the king to take the boy home? Why? / Why not?

9 **Look at the letters. Write the words.**

a c e a r g r i

1 Puss ran in front of the _carriage_.

c t l a e s

2 "Who lives in that _____?"
Puss asked the men.

r e g o

3 "Our master lives there. He is
an _____," said the men.

c i g m a

4 "Can ogres do _____?"
Puss asked.

n o l i

5 "Of course! Look!" the ogre said.
And he changed into a _____.

10 **Match the two parts of the sentences.**

1 The king's carriage left, and

2 Puss asked the men,

3 The men answered,

4 "He is an ogre,"

5 Puss ran to the castle, and

a said the men.

b Puss spoke to the men.

c "Our master lives there."

d the ogre came to the door.

e "Who lives in that castle?"

11 **Read the questions. Write answers using the words in the box.**

> magic   lion   eat   mouse

1 Why did the ogre say, "Come in."?

He wanted to eat Puss.

2 What did Puss ask the ogre?

....

3 What did the ogre change into first?

....

4 What did Puss ask him to change into?

....

12 Order the story. Write 1—5.

.... Puss heard people at the door.

.... Puss opened the door, and he saw the king, the princess, and his master.

1 The ogre changed into a mouse, and Puss jumped on it.

.... "This is my master's castle," said Puss.

.... Puss ate the mouse.

13 Join two sentences to make a new sentence starting with *When*.

1 The father died. He left his sons some presents.

   When the father died, he left his sons some presents.

2 Puss and his master were near a river. Puss saw the king's carriage on the road.

   _____

   _____

3 Puss opened the door. He saw the king, the princess, and his master.

   _____

   _____

14 **Choose the best answer.**

1 The princess and Puss's master

   a were happy together.

   b were not happy together.

2 The king was happy because

   a his daughter married a rich man.

   b his daughter had a clever cat.

3 Puss was happy because

   a he met the king.

   b he made money for his master.

4 The princess was happy because

   a she lived in an ogre's castle.

   b she was in love.

15 **Do the crossword.**

Down

1 A big, ugly man.

2 A very important man.

3 A very big house. Kings live here.

4 A place next to water. Food is made there.

Across

5 The daughter of a king.

6 Kings travel in this.

16 **Read the text. Complete the sentences.** 📖 ✏️ ⭐

Ogres were big men who liked to eat people. But only in stories! In many stories, ogres lived in old castles and were ugly. People had to work very hard for them. They were frightened of ogres. In the story of Puss in Boots, Puss eats the ogre when the ogre changes from a lion into a mouse.

1 Ogres were ___big men___ who liked to eat people.

2 In many stories, ogres lived in old

_____.

3 In the story, Puss eats the ogre when the ogre changes from

_____

_____.

17 Look and read. Choose the best answers.

1 Puss saw some men
   a walking.
   b working.

2 Puss said to the men, "Please say that the Lord of Carrabas is your
   a master."
   b king."

3 "Who do you work for?" said the king
   a when he saw the cat.
   b when he saw the men.

4 The men said that they worked
   a for the ogre.
   b for the Lord of Carrabas.

Level 3

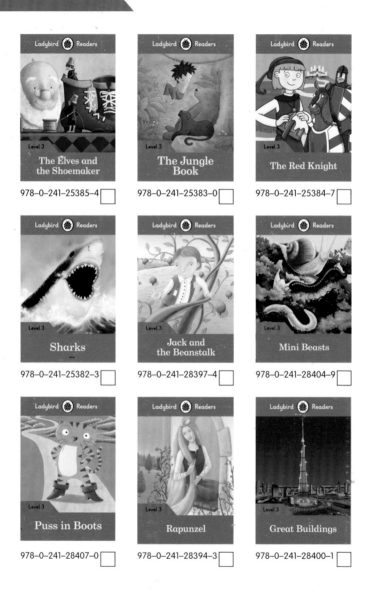

The Elves and the Shoemaker	**The Jungle Book**	**The Red Knight**
978–0–241–25385–4	978–0–241–25383–0	978–0–241–25384–7
Sharks	**Jack and the Beanstalk**	**Mini Beasts**
978–0–241–25382–3	978–0–241–28397–4	978–0–241–28404–9
Puss in Boots	**Rapunzel**	**Great Buildings**
978–0–241–28407–0	978–0–241–28394–3	978–0–241–28400–1

Now you're ready for Level 4!